Noah's Ark

For Joanna

Cinderella • Kaye Umansky
The Emperor's New Clothes • Kaye Umansky
Beauty and the Beast • Jacqueline Wilson
The Christmas Story • David Wood

Published 1997 by
A & C Black (Publishers) Limited
35 Bedford Row, London WC1R 4JH

ISBN 0-7136-4340-4

A CIP catalogue record for this book is
available from the British Library.

Series Advisor: Prue Goodwin
                Reading and Language Information Centre
                The University of Reading

Photoset in New Century Schoolbook.

Printed in Great Britain by
Hillman Printers (Frome) Ltd, Frome, Somerset.

Performance
For permission to give a public performance of **Noah's Ark**
at which an admission charge is made, please write to
Caroline Sheldon Literary Agency, 71 Hillgate Place,
London W8 7SS. You do not need permission if you do not
plan to charge an entry fee for the performance.

Noah's Ark

Kaye Umansky

Illustrated by Tessa Richardson-Jones

A & C BLACK • LONDON

Contents

A Letter from the Playwright

It was many years ago that I put on a primary school production of *Noah's Ark* - but I still remember it as one of my favourites. It is a simple story with plenty of drama. It doesn't require complicated costumes or many changes of scenery. It has the advantage of accommodating a great number of children - always a consideration if you are looking for an end-of-term production to involve a large part of the school.

Also, I had a wonderful Noah. She - yes, Noah was played by a girl - was on stage throughout the entire play. She wasn't, ordinarily, especially noticeable - nor did she shine in any other area of school activity. But on stage, she was Noah. She had a real presence as an actress. She gained a lot from the experience, both in maturity and confidence, which was very rewarding to see. Noah is a demanding as well as an exciting role, but she rose to the challenge admirably.

Please feel at liberty to use this play in any way that suits your needs. You may wish to put on a full scale production, as I did, or you may prefer to use it to read or perform individual scenes in the classroom. If you do decide to use scenes from the play to read aloud, you might find it helpful to talk to the children about the story and the main characters first (see pages 42 - 43).

After that, you could point out to the children that reading a play is different from reading a story and explain the idea of speaking dialogue in character. You could introduce them to the idea that lines are spoken in different tones of voice - and that the characters should sound like real people. Some explanation will help the children to understand more clearly what a play is, and to enjoy it all the more.

The script is a basis to work from. But it is not sacred! By all means, add extra lines, new jokes and different songs if you would like to do so. If you find that you need to expand the number of speaking parts, then the Jeerers' lines may be divided up among a large number of children. You can add as many animals to the cast as your ark will hold. Do experiment, change things, adapt - but, above all, have fun!

Good luck!

Characters In Order Of Appearance

Noah
The Boys: Shem
            Ham
            Japheth
The Girls: Ruth
           Rachel
           Rebecca
Mrs Noah
God
Jeerer One
Jeerer Two
Jeerer Three

The Animals: Elephants
             Lions
             Tigers
             Giraffes
             Rabbits
             Snakes
             Crocodiles
             Frogs
             (add more if you wish)
The Storm Dancers
The Raven
The Dove

List of Scenes and their Locations

Prologue - God speaks to Noah   : *On A Mountain Top*

Act 1

Scene 1 - Great News!   : *Mrs Noah's Kitchen*
Scene 2 - Making The Ark   : *The Building Site*
Scene 3 - The Animals Arrive : *Outside the Ark*

[Interval if desired]

Act 2

Scene 1 - The Storm   : *Outside the Ark*
Scene 2 - Down In The Hold   : *Aboard the Ark*
Scene 3 - On Deck   : *Aboard the Ark*
Scene 4 - Land At Last   : *Outside the Ark*

The playing time is approximately 45 minutes without an interval.

Prologue - God Speaks to Noah

On A Mountain Top. There is a tree stump at the front of the stage. We hear thunder. NOAH enters carrying a staff. He walks to the front of the stage.

NOAH: *(to audience)* Ah. Good. There you are. I was hoping you'd come, because I've got a story to tell you. A story with quite a few scary bits in it. Storms at sea. God getting angry. That sort of thing. But there are funny bits too. And bags of animal interest. You don't mind if I sit down, do you? I'm getting too old to climb mountains. *(NOAH sits on the tree stump.)* Now then. The story. You do <u>like</u> stories, I hope? I know my boys used to, when they were small. Of course, they're bigger now. All grown up and married. See them?

(SHEM, HAM, JAPHETH, RUTH, RACHEL and REBECCA enter. Lights up on the group. NOAH points to them. They pose solemnly as if for a photograph.)

NOAH: Shem, Ham and Japheth. Those are their names. Smile, boys.

(The BOYS smile.)

NOAH: And those are their wives – Ruth, Rachel and Rebecca. The three R's, I call them. Wave, girls.

(The GIRLS wave.)

NOAH: All right, children, you can go now. But not for long, mind. I shall be needing you shortly.

(The BOYS and the GIRLS exit.)

NOAH: I want to start properly, at the beginning. And there's quite a lot to tell, so I'd better be quick about it before Mrs Noah calls me in for tea. She's fussy about mealtimes, is Mrs Noah. There she is, look.

(Lights up on MRS NOAH. NOAH points to her. She is peeling potatoes.)

MRS NOAH: Listen to him. Doesn't he go on?
         (to NOAH) Get a move on, you silly old thing,
         it's nearly tea-time.

(Lights down on MRS NOAH. She exits.)

NOAH: You heard her. I'd better get cracking.
         It all began like this...

(There is a loud rumble of thunder. Startled, NOAH jumps to his feet. We hear the voice of GOD from off stage.)

GOD: *(loudly)* Noah!

NOAH: Aaah! Who's that?

(GOD enters.)

GOD: It is I, Noah. Your God.

NOAH: Oh my Go'... Goodness.

(NOAH sinks into a kneeling position.)

GOD: I have been thinking, Noah. I am not pleased
         with the way things have been going.
         You humans have become selfish and wicked.
         You don't care about each other any more.
         It is time to wipe the slate and start again.

NOAH: But – Lord. All that time that you spent on the Creation.
         It seems such a waste.

GOD: Do not question me, Noah. I have decided.
         In one week's time, I shall send rain.
         Rain like you have never seen before. For forty days
         and forty nights the rain will fall. The waters
         will cover the face of the earth.
         And all will perish.

NOAH: Isn't that a bit extreme?

GOD: You and your family I shall save. You are
                   the chosen ones. You must build a great ark,
                   Noah. Make it three hundred cubits long,
                   fifty cubits across and thirty cubits high.

(NOAH scrabbles in the pocket of his robe, produces a pad and pencil and scribbles furiously.)

GOD: Have you got that?

NOAH: Nearly. How high was it again?

GOD: Thirty cubits.

NOAH: *(writing)* Thirty cubits...

GOD: Into this ark, I want you to put two animals of every sort.

NOAH: What – even elephants?

GOD: *(firmly)* Especially elephants. I'm rather proud of them.
                   One of my better efforts, elephants.

(NOAH sighs and writes it down.)

NOAH: Elephants. Right, I've got that. And after I've got all these
                   animals into the ark – er – what happens then, Lord?

GOD: Then, Noah – you will place yourselves in my keeping.

(There is a thunderclap. GOD exits.)

NOAH: *(to audience)* By which He meant, I think,
                   I'd better hope for the best.

(NOAH exits.)

Act 1, Scene 1 – Great News!

Mrs Noah's Kitchen. There is a great bustle going on. RUTH and RACHEL are preparing the meal. REBECCA is scrubbing the floor. MRS NOAH presides over them all.

MRS NOAH: Pass me the salt, would you, Ruth?

RUTH: Right away, Mum.

MRS NOAH: Have you laid the table, Rachel?

RACHEL: Nearly, Mum.

MRS NOAH: Finished scrubbing that floor, Rebecca? I want to be able to eat off it, mind.

REBECCA: But I thought we were eating off the table...

MRS NOAH: *(sternly)* Just do it.

(REBECCA sighs and continues scrubbing the floor.)

MRS NOAH: Ah, what it is to be content. In me own kitchen in me own little house. Three big boys, all grown up and nicely settled and three daughters-in-law to boss around. I couldn't ask for anything more.

(MRS NOAH sighs contentedly. She looks around her, surveying her spotless kitchen in an approving way. Suddenly, she looks sharply at the floor. She has noticed a speck of dirt.)

MRS NOAH: Do that again, Rebecca, there's marks.

REBECCA: Oh, but Mum...

MRS NOAH: Who's the boss in <u>this</u> kitchen?

THE GIRLS: *(resignedly)* You are, Mum.

MRS NOAH: Good girls. That's the <u>right</u> answer!

(THE GIRLS sing the following song to the tune of The Sailor's Hornpipe.)

SHE'S THE BOSS ROUND HERE

1. She's the boss round here,
    And it's really pretty clear
    Mrs Noah is the one
    That the folks all fear,
    With her elbows deep in flour,
    She can really make you cower,
    She's the one with all the power,
    She's the boss round here.

2. She's the undisputed leader of the soup tureen,
    You no sooner put your feet up with a magazine,
    Then she bustles in the kitchen shouting 'Clean! Clean! Clean!'
    Yes, we know that Mrs Noah is the boss round here.

3. She's the boss round here,
    And you mustn't interfere
    Or you'll get a telling off
    That is quite severe,
    In the kitchen she's the skipper,
    Better button up your lip or
    She will hit you with a kipper,
    She's the boss round here.

4. It's very true to say we are beneath her thumb,
    If you're thinking of promotion, well, forget it, chum,
    Better buckle down and scrub a bit, 'cause here comes Mum -
    Yes we know that Mrs Noah is the boss round here!

MRS NOAH: Yes, I'm the boss all right. And don't you forget it.

(SHEM, HAM and JAPHETH enter.)

SHEM: What a day. My back's breaking from all that ploughing!
                   The earth's so dry, its like rock.

RUTH: Here. Have some water.

(RUTH takes a jug of water to SHEM, HAM and JAPHETH and mimes pouring them cups of water from it. They mime drinking.)

HAM: I've never known it so hot. Even the donkey had to go and lie down, poor old thing. It took nine carrots to persuade it back to work.

JAPHETH: You spoil that donkey, Ham. The way you treat it, you'd think it was made of solid gold.

HAM: Well, it is. It's a nine carrot donkey.

SHEM: *(to MRS NOAH)* Is tea ready? I'm starving.

MRS NOAH: Just about. Have any of you seen your father?

HAM: Went off on one of his nature rambles up the mountain, I think.

JAPHETH: It looked like there was a bit of a storm brewing up there. He's probably sheltering.

MRS NOAH: Tch, tch. He'll be late again, no doubt, all on account of some rare buttercup or dirty old bird's nest. And he knows I like meals on time. What a nuisance he is.

NOAH: *(off stage)* Mother? It's me! I'm back!

JAPHETH: There he is now.

(Enter NOAH waving his notebook excitedly.)

NOAH: Ah good, everyone's here. Gather round, I've got some incredible news. I've just had the most amazing experience! I was up in the mountains, and...

MRS NOAH: Noah! Wipe your feet! You're soaking wet, just look at you. Rebecca, love, get a cloth and wipe the floor.

REBECCA: But I've just done the floor...

MRS NOAH: <u>Now.</u>

(REBECCA obeys.)

RUTH: How come you're so wet, Dad?

RACHEL: Did you fall in the water trough?

NOAH: I got caught in a small storm, if you must know. And if
              you think this is wet, just you wait until a week's time...
              (to REBECCA) Ah, stop your fussing, Rebecca.
              This is no time to be fooling about with housework.
              We've got real, important things to do.

MRS NOAH: What <u>are</u> you talking about, Noah?

NOAH: I'm talking about rain, Mother. Forty days and
              forty nights of it. Not a glimmer of a let-up.
              Whoosh! Splosh! Rain.

SHEM: Who says?

NOAH: God says.

HAM: Oh yes? And I suppose He told you personally?

NOAH: Well yes, He did, as a matter of fact.

MRS NOAH: Get along with you and your nonsense.
              Keeping us all waiting for tea. Ruth, dish up the soup
              before it gets cold.

NOAH: Hold it right there, Ruth. The soup can wait.
              Mother, have I ever lied to you?

MRS NOAH: Well, no, but...

NOAH: Then believe me now. God spoke to me on the mountain.
              He told me that in one week's time, the clouds
              will open. There will be terrible floods, and everyone

	will drown.
HAM:	Pity I didn't keep up my swimming lessons, then.

(Everyone laughs except NOAH and MRS NOAH.)

NOAH:	*(angrily)* Don't laugh! Now listen to me, because we don't have much time. We have to build a special kind of boat, called an ark. I've got all the dimensions written down, He was very specific. And when it's finished, we have to bring together two of every kind of animal and herd them aboard.
SHEM:	Oh, is <u>that</u> all?
JAPHETH:	Dad, have you any idea what you're talking about? It's statistically impossible. If you had the slightest idea about maths...
HAM:	Rachel, send for the men in white coats. Dad's finally gone crazy.
MRS NOAH:	Be quiet, you boys. I believe your father's serious.
NOAH:	Never more serious in my life. God spoke to me. 'Noah,' He said, 'It's your job to save the animals. Two of every kind.'
RACHEL:	What – even elephants?
NOAH:	Yes. He was most definite about elephants.
HAM:	Wow! Elephants! Heavy!
RUTH:	Giraffes?
NOAH:	Certainly giraffes.
SHEM:	That's a tall order.
REBECCA:	What about rabbits?

NOAH: Rabbits too.

JAPHETH: There won't be two of them for long!

RUTH: *(shuddering)* Not snakes, I hope?

RACHEL: Or crocodiles?

REBECCA: Or frogs. Yuck!

NOAH: Yes, yes, yes. Two of everything. I keep telling you.

MRS NOAH: Now, let me get this straight. You want us to leave our lovely little house and move into a Do-It-Yourself outsized houseboat with a lot of smelly animals.

NOAH: Correct.

MRS NOAH: And then it's going to rain. For forty days and nights. And everyone will drown except us.

NOAH: Yes.

MRS NOAH: And God told you this?

NOAH: Yes.

MRS NOAH: Oh well. That's that, then. Better get packing.

(There is great anxiety among the others.)

REBECCA: But Mum! Tell him.

MRS NOAH: No point. Not once he's got the bit between his teeth. It's the practical side that bothers me. How are we supposed to feed all these creatures? Once we've got them aboard?

NOAH: *(vaguely)* Some sort of system with buckets, perhaps?

	I was hoping that would be your department, Mother.
MRS NOAH:	I had a feeling he was going to say that.
NOAH:	I'm sure you'll rise to the challenge. Come on,
	boys, follow me – there's work to be done.
	We must start by cutting down some trees,
	and then we have to order some tar...

(NOAH exits, followed by SHEM, HAM and JAPHETH, all talking at once.)

SHEM:	Wait a minute, Dad, this is ridiculous...
HAM:	We don't know the first thing about ship building...
JAPHETH:	You've got to draw up proper plans, Dad, you can't just
	stick a few planks together and hope for the best...

(MRS NOAH is left with RUTH, RACHEL and REBECCA.)

MRS NOAH:	Hmm. Two of every kind, eh? That's a lot
	of mouths to feed. Take a bit of organising.
RUTH:	What shall we do, Mum?
MRS NOAH:	*(rolling up her sleeves)* What do you think?
	We make lists. It takes a woman to get things organised.
	Bring me a pencil and paper, Ruth. Rebecca, find
	that book about animals and what they eat.
	And get those lamps lit, Rachel. Tonight we're going
	to burn a lot of midnight oil!

(MRS NOAH, RUTH, RACHEL and REBECCA exit.)

Act 1, Scene 2 – Making the Ark

The Building Site. NOAH enters and walks to the front of the stage.

NOAH: *(to the audience)* I suppose you think I was a bit hard
on them? It must have come as a bit of a shock.
But what was I supposed to say? There's no way
of breaking a thing like that gently. But they're
a good lot. They rallied round. Well, they had to.
I had my orders from on high, you see.

(Lights up. There is a carpenter's bench at the front of the stage. SHEM, HAM, JAPHETH, RUTH, RACHEL and REBECCA enter carrying parts of the ark with them. They assemble the ark on stage. Then they mime sawing up pieces of wood, hammering nails into the ark and painting it. They are being watched by a sneering crowd of onlookers.)

(Everyone sings the following song to the tune of The Hokey-Cokey.)

THAT'S HOW YOU BUILD AN ARK

1.   You stick a nail in here,
A nail in there,
You bang your thumb
And you jump up in the air,
You get up in the morning
And you work till dark,
That's how you build an ark.

      Oooh, Mother is it raining?
Oooh, Mother is it raining?
Oooh Mother is it raining?
Gotta get done before the rain comes down.

2.   You put the paint on here,
The paint on there,
Splish splosh, splish splosh,
Paint it everywhere,
You put a bit of tar along the water mark,
That's how you build an ark.

Oooh, Mother is it raining?
Oooh, Mother is it raining?
Oooh Mother is it raining?
Gotta get done before the rain comes down.

3.   You saw the wood just here,
And then just there,
You stop to shake
All the sawdust from your hair,
You're running out of energy,
You can't produce a spark,
That's how you build an ark.

Oooh, Mother is it raining?
Oooh, Mother is it raining?
Oooh Mother is it raining?
Gotta get done before the rain comes down.

JEERER ONE: You're mad, you lot.

JEERER TWO: Bonkers. What d'you want to build a ship in your back yard for?

JEERER THREE: I've heard of a ship in a bottle, but not in a garden.

SHEM: You won't be laughing when the rain starts, mate.

JEERER THREE: Ooh! Mummy, I'm fwightened!

JEERER ONE: What are you talking about, rain! It's the hottest it's been in years. There's not a cloud in the sky, look.

JEERER TWO: Bonkers, the lot of 'em.

SHEM: I'm gonna get him...

RUTH: Ignore them, Shem. They're just trying to wind us up.

REBECCA: Haven't you got anything better to do?

JEERER ONE: What, like, go and order an umbrella before they all run out?

RACHEL:	No. She means why not give us a hand instead of hanging about making stupid remarks.
JEERER THREE:	Stupid? Well, I like that. We're only trying to keep you entertained while you're working, aren't we, boys?
JEERER ONE:	Dead right. Knock knock!
TWO and THREE:	Who's there?
JEERER ONE:	Noah.
TWO and THREE:	Noah who?
JEERER ONE:	Noah good place to sail a boat? I just happen to have one in my back yard.

(The JEERERS fall about laughing.)

JAPHETH:	Look, why don't you just clear off and leave us alone.
SHEM:	That's right. Or we'll make you, won't we, boys?
THE GIRLS:	*(together)* Oh no you <u>won't</u>.
RUTH:	Violence never solves anything. You know what Dad always says. Never argue with a quarrelsome person. Answer him with soft words.
RACHEL:	Which'll make him crosser than anything.
REBECCA:	Ruth's right, Shem. Thumping people doesn't achieve anything.
SHEM:	It'd achieve a black eye on him for a start.
JEERER ONE:	Oh yeah?
THE BOYS:	<u>YEAH!</u>

(The JEERERS and the BOYS get ready to fight each other. NOAH enters with his arms full of plans.)

NOAH:	Whoa, whoa. What's going on here?

SHEM:	They're taking the micky again.

JEERER ONE:	Morning, Mr Noah. We were just saying. Lovely day for a sail...

JEERER TWO:	If you're bonkers, that is!

JEERER THREE:	Lovely boat, though. Shame he doesn't live near the coast.

(The JEERERS exit, laughing and singing 'Row, Row, Row Your Boat'.)

SHEM:	I'll get 'em, see if I don't.

NOAH:	Shem, Shem. Calm down. Don't waste your time on the likes of them. There's work to be done.

SHEM:	*(sighing)* I know, I know. I just hope it's all worth it. Pass me that hammer, Ham.

(HAM passes SHEM the hammer. SHEM knocks in a nail and hits his thumb.)

SHEM:	Ouch!

(The work starts again. NOAH moves to the front of the stage and addresses the audience.)

NOAH:	It wasn't an easy week. I had my work cut out to keep their spirits up. Mrs Noah in particular suffered a great deal. It's not easy to build a ship in your back yard without creating a bit of dust – and you know how fussy she is. But she did her best, I'll give her that.

(MRS NOAH enters. She is carrying at least four or five buckets.)

MRS NOAH: It's all very well for him. Get buckets, he says.
Fill 'em up with the things animals like.
Well, I've got buckets all right. I've got buckets
as far as the eye can see. I dream about buckets.
Buckets of carrots, buckets of oats, buckets of bird seed.
I've yet to find out what crocodiles eat, but I've got
a nasty feeling you can't put it in a bucket...

(MRS NOAH exits, leaving the buckets on stage. The BOYS and the GIRLS exit, carrying the carpenter's bench off stage with them.)

NOAH: No, it wasn't easy. But we kept at it, ignoring the taunts
of our neighbours. And, with God's help, we did it!
We made an ark, exactly to His instructions.
Would you like to see it? You would?
Well, good - because here's one we made earlier!

(NOAH points to the ark proudly, and then exits.)

Act 1, Scene 3 – The Animals Arrive

Outside the Ark. Lights up. We hear a burst of dramatic, triumphal music. After a minute, MRS NOAH, HAM, SHEM, JAPHETH, RUTH, RACHEL and REBECCA enter, and gaze at the completed ark. A minute or two later, NOAH enters.

HAM: Well, Dad, that's it. The last nail's gone in. What do you think of it?

(There is a pause while NOAH inspects the ark.)

NOAH: I think it's perfect. Well done, everyone. I'm proud of you.

(A cheer goes up.)

RUTH: Aren't you forgetting something, Dad?

NOAH: What's that, Ruth?

RUTH: The animals. Just a little detail.

RACHEL: According to you, the rain's due to start in about quarter of an hour. You've left it a bit late to scour all four corners of the earth for two of every kind, haven't you?

REBECCA: You've got to be practical. Hasn't he, Mum?

JAPHETH: They're right, Dad. We have left it a bit tight.

NOAH: Have faith, children. Something will turn up. Miracles do happen, you know.

MRS NOAH: If I've made up all those buckets for nothing, you're going to need a miracle all right...

RUTH: Ssssh.

MRS NOAH: Don't you shush me, Miss.

RUTH: I can hear something coming, Mum!

RACHEL: She's right.

REBECCA: It sounds like a lot of hooves...

SHEM: Well, I'll be... It's the animals! They're coming!

NOAH: You see? You've got to have faith!

(We hear a musical march as the ANIMALS enter, two by two. Each pair is introduced in turn by one of the GIRLS or BOYS, in the manner of a circus ringmaster. Each pair of ANIMALS parades into the ark in a different way, according to what kind of animal they are.)

SHEM: Ladies and gentlemen! Without further ado,
                   may I introduce the ELEPHANTS!

HAM: Put your hands together for the kings of the jungle,
                   ladies and gentlemen - the LIONS!

JAPHETH: Let's give a big warm, biblical welcome to
                   the TIGERS!

RUTH: Let's hear it for the GIRAFFES!

REBECCA: And who else but your own, your very own – RABBITS!

RACHEL: The SNAKES, ladies and gentlemen!

(The introductions continue in this fashion until all the ANIMALS have entered the ark except the CROCODILES and the FROGS.)

MRS NOAH: Oh no! I knew it! Here come the crocodiles.
                   (To the CROCODILES) Just don't expect much
                   in the way of catering, d'you hear?

(The CROCODILES enter.)

SHEM: Is that it?

HAM: Not quite.

JAPHETH: Last, but not least, the little green fellas
                        – the FROGS, ladies and gentlemen!

*(The FROGS enter the ark. MR and MRS NOAH, the BOYS and the GIRLS line
up and pass the buckets into the ark.)*

SHEM: That's it. They're all in, plus the provisions.

RUTH: What do we do now, Dad?

NOAH: Now we wait. For rain.

*(NOAH, MRS NOAH, the GIRLS and the BOYS stand with hands outstretched
expectantly, waiting for the first drops of rain. The ANIMALS crouch down
behind the ark. Lights down.)*

INTERVAL

Act 2, Scene 1 – The Storm

Outside the Ark. In the darkness, we hear thunder rumbling and the sound of the first drops of rain beginning to fall. Gradually the lights come up. NOAH, MRS NOAH, the GIRLS and the BOYS stand with hands outstretched, watching the sky.

(Everyone sings the following song as a round, to the tune of London's Burning.)

I CAN FEEL IT!

> I can feel it,
> I can feel it,
> On my face and
> On my shoulders,
> Cold rain!
> Wet rain!
> Falling softly
> From the heavens.

(The sound of the rain increases. We hear the voice of GOD from off stage.)

GOD: Now is the time, Noah! Take your family and enter the ark
           – for the windows of heaven are open. The rain has come.
           The rivers will swell and burst their banks,
           and the seas will rise and take back the land.
           The waters will cover the mountains, and all
           will perish – for that is my command. Go into the ark,
           Noah. Now is the time. Save yourselves!

NOAH: In, quickly! You heard Him!

(MRS NOAH, the BOYS and the GIRLS enter the ark. NOAH enters last.)

NOAH: *(to GOD)* I just hope you know what you're doing!

(NOAH goes into the ark and mimes closing the door. Lights up. We hear music. The STORM DANCERS come on stage and begin their dance. The storm increases. The terrified JEERERS come on stage and are buffeted by the waves. They struggle, but are dragged down below the water. They crawl off stage. Slowly, the storm music dies away, leaving just the pattering of rain. The STORM DANCERS end their dance. They exit. Lights down.)

Act 2, Scene 2 – Down In The Hold

Aboard the Ark. It is dark. The RAVEN and the DOVE creep quietly on stage and join the ANIMALS crouched behind the ark. We hear the sound of rhythmic stamping of feet, getting louder. There are wild cries from the ANIMALS as the lights come up. The ANIMALS stand up and stamp their feet in time to their chant.

ANIMALS:

Nowhere to run!
Nowhere to hide!
Days and nights
Cooped up inside!
We're all cramped up!
The food is bad!
Is it any wonder that
We're all going mad!

All going mad!
All going mad!
Is it any wonder that
We're all going mad!

FROGS and
CROCODILES:

Nowhere to crawl,

DOVE and RAVEN:

Nowhere to fly,

GIRAFFES, LIONS,
and TIGERS:

No green grass!
No blue sky!

ANIMALS:

The days are long
And the nights are sad,
Is it any wonder that
We're all going mad?

All going mad!
All going mad!
Is it any wonder that
We're all going mad?

Can't get out!
Can't go back!
It's all too much
And we're starting to crack,
Give us back the freedom
We once had!
Is it any wonder that
We're all going mad!

All going mad!
All going mad!
Is it any wonder that
WE'RE ALL GOING MAD!

(The ANIMALS break into a wild chorus of growls, hisses, angry twitterings and trumpeting noises. Enter MRS NOAH, RUTH, RACHEL and REBECCA – with the buckets of food.)

MRS NOAH: All right, all right, that's quite enough from you lot.
Give them their food, girls, that'll keep them quiet
for a bit.

(She sighs deeply. RUTH, RACHEL and REBECCA distribute food to the ANIMALS. The CROCODILES refuse their food and the ELEPHANTS examine their buns with displeasure. All the ANIMALS crouch down behind the ark again.)

RACHEL: The crocodiles are still refusing to eat, Mum.

MRS NOAH: I told you they'd be trouble. What about the elephants?

REBECCA: They don't seem keen. These buns are a bit stale.

MRS NOAH: Well, they'll have to make the best of it. Same as the rest of us.
(to the ANIMALS) It's not just you lot that are suffering,
you know. We're all sick of the food. We've been living
on potatoes for the last three days. In fact, we're sick
of everything. Oh, to be able to stretch me legs out
in front of a blazing fire.

RUTH: It's fresh vegetables that I miss.

RACHEL: With me, it's the sunshine.

REBECCA: I'd give anything for a nice, juicy orange that isn't past its sell-by date.

(They all sigh. Enter SHEM, HAM and JAPHETH.)

SHEM: Ah, there you are. We've been looking for you. What are you sitting down for? Isn't it time someone organised supper?

RUTH: *(sharply)* Oh yes? Well, what does sir fancy? A nice drop of potato soup, perhaps?

REBECCA: Or perhaps you'd like soup with potato in?

RACHEL: Or maybe, just for a change, some cooked lumps of potato floating in hot water in a kind of soup-like way?

HAM: Oh no. Not potato soup <u>again</u>.

JAPHETH: Boring!

SHEM: Isn't there anything else?

MRS NOAH: No. And you should be grateful for that. It won't be long before we run out of potatoes. Then you'll really have something to complain about.

RUTH: Anyway, I don't see why we should have to cook your supper. We're busy enough feeding the animals.

RACHEL: That's right. Do it yourself for a change.

HAM: Well, that's a cheek! Who does all the mucking out round here?

JAPHETH: Not to mention all the repairs. Ham and I were up till midnight last night fixing the leaks, weren't we, Ham?

HAM:	Yep. And now we're hungry.
SHEM:	That's right. We do all the manly jobs. It's the women's job to do the cooking.
RUTH:	*(crossly)* One day, all that will change.
MRS NOAH:	I wouldn't rely on it, dear.

(Enter NOAH.)

NOAH:	What's all this? Raised voices?

(Everyone speaks together.)

MRS NOAH:	It's time you spoke to those boys, Noah, they're getting a darn sight too cheeky...
RUTH:	It's not fair, Dad, they're complaining because we haven't cooked supper.
RACHEL:	As if we haven't got enough to do!
REBECCA:	It's not <u>our</u> fault if there's only potatoes.
SHEM:	We've had a hard day's work, and now they're refusing to cook!
HAM:	Man cannot live on potato soup alone!
JAPHETH:	We're doing all the work round here and all they can do is complain!
NOAH	Stop! Stop! Calm down, all of you. All this arguing isn't getting us anywhere.
SHEM:	So? We're not going anywhere anyway. We've been stuck in the ark for over five weeks, and all we've seen is water.
HAM:	There's nowhere to go, Dad. You might as well admit it. We're stuck on this ark forever – and it's all your doing. We might as well have stayed where we were and taken

JAPHETH: our chances. At least the end would have been quick. The whole world's underwater. And don't keep telling us we must have faith. What good is faith, when there's nothing to eat? You can't eat faith.

RUTH: And if you could, you could cook it yourself!

RACHEL and
REBECCA: Hear hear!

(MRS NOAH, the GIRLS and the BOYS all fall into a sulk. Everyone is glaring at each other. NOAH gives a sigh, and turns away from them to address the audience.)

NOAH: It's a long time, forty days and forty nights.
Tempers got frayed. I did my best to keep the peace but I'm not God. I can't work miracles.
(He gazes at his family regretfully.) I hate to see them this way. If you'll excuse me, I think I'll go up on deck for a bit. Get a bit of fresh air.

(Sadly, NOAH exits.)

EVERYONE: All going mad!
All going mad!
Is it any wonder that
<u>WE'RE ALL GOING MAD!</u>

(MRS NOAH, the BOYS and the GIRLS exit. Lights down.)

Act 2, Scene 3 – On Deck

Aboard the Ark. Lights up. We hear the sound of rain falling. Enter NOAH.
He walks to the front of the stage and mimes looking out to sea, shading his eyes
and looking out across the audience. MRS NOAH enters.

MRS NOAH: Noah?

NOAH: Ah. There you are, Mother.

MRS NOAH: Look at you, you're getting soaked. Here.
Share my umbrella.

(She joins him at the front of the stage. Together they scan the horizon.)

MRS NOAH: Still no sign of land.

NOAH: No. No sign.

MRS NOAH: It's not your fault, Noah. Don't go blaming yourself.
You did it for the best.

NOAH: I'm sorry about the house. And everything.

MRS NOAH: *(sighing)* I know.

NOAH: Is there no more food?

MRS NOAH: Barely enough potatoes for another day. Then it's all gone
except the elephants' buns. I haven't told the children yet.
Or the elephants.

NOAH: If only there was a sign. Something to tell us that God
hasn't forgotten us...

(The sound of the rain begins to die away.)

MRS NOAH: Noah?

NOAH: *(continuing)* Nothing major, just a little hint
that things will improve...

MRS NOAH: Noah!

NOAH: A shape in the clouds, or something simple like
a burning bush...

MRS NOAH: NOAH!

NOAH: Mmm?

MRS NOAH: It's stopped.

NOAH: What has?

MRS NOAH: The rain! Don't you see? It's stopped!

(NOAH stretches out his hand, hardly daring to believe it.)

NOAH: You're right! This is it, Mother – the sign
we've been waiting for! God be praised!
(He lowers the umbrella and calls.) Children!

SHEM: *(off stage)* What is it now?

NOAH: Come up here this minute! I've got something to show you.

HAM: *(off stage)* But they're making us peel potatoes...

MRS NOAH: That's my girls.

NOAH: Never mind the potatoes. Come here this minute.
And, Shem! Pick up a penguin on your way up.
I need it for an experiment.

MRS NOAH: I should make it a raven if I were you, dear.
(to the audience) He's always had a poor grasp
of natural history.

NOAH: She's right. As always. Shem! Make that a raven!

SHEM: *(off stage)* But, Dad...

MRS NOAH:	Now! Do as your father tells you.
JAPHETH:	*(off stage)* Hang on, we're finding our umbrellas...
NOAH:	Forget the umbrellas! Don't you understand? It's stopped raining!

(Enter HAM, JAPHETH, RUTH, RACHEL and REBECCA at a run.)

HAM:	Did you say it's stopped raining?
JAPHETH:	He's right! Look, there's a patch of blue sky!
RUTH:	Where?
RACHEL:	Over there, look!
REBECCA:	I can see it! I can!

(Enter SHEM with the RAVEN.)

SHEM:	Here's the raven. What do I do with it?
NOAH:	Let it go, son. If there is land to be found, the bird will find it.
SHEM:	Off you go! Fly! Bring us back a sign!

(The RAVEN flies away and exits. MRS NOAH, the GIRLS and the BOYS watch it go and stand with arms outstretched waving goodbye.)

NOAH:	And so we waited long hours for the raven to return. But it never did.

(MRS NOAH, the GIRLS and the BOYS slump in disappointment. NOAH notices them.)

NOAH:	Hey! We mustn't lose hope. We've come too far to give in to despair now. Ham! Go below and fetch me a... what d'you call it? White, with feathers...?

(He turns for help to MRS NOAH.)

MRS NOAH: I think a dove would fit the bill very nicely.

NOAH: Thank you, Mother. A dove, Ham. Quickly!

(HAM exits.)

SHEM: What's the point? If the raven didn't return,
what makes you think the dove will?

MRS NOAH: Stop your arguing, boy. You're getting too cheeky by half.
Your father's been right all along.

NOAH: *(to the audience)* She has a sharp tongue, does Mrs Noah,
but she's always on my side, do you notice?
And she's very informed about animals.

MRS NOAH: Although I'm still not sure what crocodiles eat.

(Enter HAM with the DOVE.)

NOAH: Let it go, son. Fly away, my little feathered friend.
All our hopes go with you.

(The DOVE flies away and exits. Again, MRS NOAH, the GIRLS and the BOYS stand with their arms outstretched, waving goodbye.)

NOAH: Again, we waited. Time seemed to stand still as we
watched the skies, hoping for a glimpse of those small,
strong wings. Our eyes ached and our spirits reached
their lowest ebb. And, just when it seemed that all
was lost – the miracle happened.

SHEM: Dad! I think I can see it! See that speck in the sky?

JAPHETH: He's right! It's coming back – and it's got
something in its beak.

RACHEL: It's an olive branch!

(The DOVE enters with an olive branch, which it presents to NOAH.)

NOAH: You know what this means, don't you?

ALL: Land! Hooray!

(There is great joy. Everyone starts to sing the following song, to the tune of When The Saints Go Marching In.)

WE'VE REACHED THE SHORE

1.   We've reached the shore!
      We've reached the shore!
      There's a new world to explore!
      We'll say goodbye to all that water,
      And we'll walk on land once more.

2.   We're home and dry,
      We're home and dry,
      And high above is bright blue sky,
      We'll say goodbye to all that water,
      For at last, we're home and dry.

3.   We're safe at last!
      We're safe at last!
      Now the storm is safely past,
      We'll say goodbye to all that water,
      For we're home and safe at last.

(Lights down.)

Act 2, Scene 4 – Land At Last

Outside the Ark. NOAH walks to the front of the stage.

NOAH: *(to the audience)* And so, after forty days and nights, the ark came to rest on a mountain top and the waters receded. And that's when God spoke to me again.

GOD: *(from off stage)* Noah!

NOAH: Yes, Lord? I'm right here.

(GOD enters.)

GOD: You have done well, Noah. I am pleased. All the wickedness and cruelty has been washed away. You have a new world now. You can start again. It's up to you.

NOAH: Lord?

GOD: Well?

NOAH: You – er – you're not thinking of doing something like this again, are you? Frankly, I think I'm getting a bit too old for it.

GOD: You have my word, Noah. I shall not do this again. If ever you should doubt me, look to the rainbow. I leave it with you as a sign that I shall keep my promise. Behold!

(A rainbow appears.)

GOD: And, now, go forth and multiply!

(There is a fanfare. The RAVEN enters and joins the DOVE. They take their bows. Then the rest of the ANIMALS come downstage two by two, and take their bows. The JEERERS and the STORM DANCERS enter and take their bows. They are followed by SHEM and RUTH, RACHEL and HAM, REBECCA and JAPHETH, NOAH and MRS NOAH and GOD. The entire cast could sing The Animals Went In Two by Two as a finale.)

THE END

Staging

How you stage *Noah's Ark* will, of course, depend on your particular circumstances, and the facilities that are available to you. You may have a school theatre with a stage, or you may be able to create an acting area at the end of the hall, by using rostra blocks.

It is possible to stage *Noah's Ark* quite simply, using one main acting area throughout. If possible, it's a good idea to construct your acting area on two levels, with steps or a ramp in the middle, connecting the two. If you have a theatre with a fixed stage, you can build the lower level out at the front of the stage, with rostra blocks.

Most of the action of the play takes place outside the ark - and therefore on the lower level; or aboard the ark - and thus on the upper level. The construction of the ark is explained on pages 38 and 39.

However, it may be that the only space available to you is the space at the front of the classroom or in the gymnasium. Then your acting area will all be on one level. In that case, the scenes that take place outside the ark should be performed at the front of the area (downstage). The scenes that happen aboard the ark should be enacted at the rear of the acting area (upstage).

Noah's Ark doesn't require elaborate staging. It can be performed in almost any kind of space. Only one large piece of scenery (the ark) and a few props are needed to show the different locations.

Backdrops

One all-purpose backdrop is very useful for *Noah's Ark*. This backdrop should show the outline of the roof of Noah's house, which becomes the outline of the roof of the ark, later on.

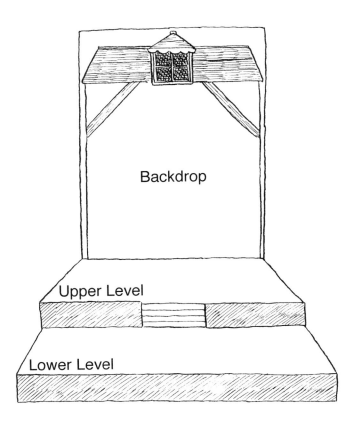

This backdrop remains in place from the beginning of Act 1, scene 1, until the end of the play. You will need to establish how to display or hang the backdrop, behind the acting area. Once you know what size it should be, you can make the backdrop by taping together a number of large sheets of paper with masking tape. Draw the shape of the roof on the backdrop first, and then colour it in.

Scenery and Props

There are seven scenes and a prologue in *Noah's Ark*. The action takes place in four different locations; firstly on a mountain top, next in Mrs Noah's kitchen, then at the building site and thereafter in and around the ark itself. Once the ark has been assembled on stage (at the beginning of Act 1, scene 2) only the ark's surroundings change - to show whether the actors are outside the ark or aboard it; on land or at sea.

Other than the ark itself, there is only one piece of scenery to make - the rainbow. The Storm Dancers create a storm at the end of Act 2, scene 1, and will need some lengths of material to use as waves. A few props will indicate the location of each scene. You will probably have your own ideas about how to make the props, but here are some suggestions.

On A Mountain Top

If you have rostra blocks, one placed on top of another will make an excellent mountain. If these are not available, Noah can simply sit at the front of the stage. He needs a sturdy tree stump to sit on. Cut out a tree stump shape from strong cardboard and paint the front of it. Attach a stool to the back of the shape as shown. Turn it round for use!

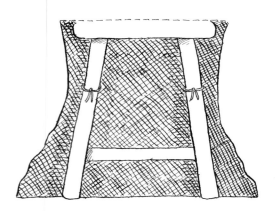

Mrs Noah's Kitchen

All that is required is a table and a chair for Mrs Noah. The table should be laid with bowls and spoons. If you wish, you can decorate the set with large storage jars, and sacks of grain. (Fill dustbin liner bags with scrunched-up balls of paper and label the bags appropriately.)

The Building Site

A carpenter's bench should be placed in front of the ark during this scene to indicate that building work is still in progress. A school bench would be suitable. One or two hammers and saws (cut out from card and covered in silver foil) and a few paint brushes in paint pots will create the building site.

Outside and Aboard the Ark

The actors playing Noah's children bring on all the separate pieces of the ark at the beginning of Act 1, scene 2, and assemble it. It remains on stage until the end of the play.

The ark is quite a large piece of scenery, but it's not difficult to make. It should be made in two halves. You will need six cardboard boxes (about 100 cm high) to make the whole ark. (You could ask your local supermarket to save six similar boxes for you.) Cover the fronts of all six boxes with plain paper or thin card.

Scenery and Props

To make the left-hand side of the ark, line up three of the boxes and draw the ark shape on the papered front of the boxes, as shown below. You could paint the ark shape to look like planks of wood. Paint on some nails and portholes too.

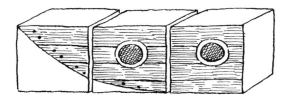

Make the right-hand side of the ark using the other three papered boxes. You will need to show the mirror-image of the left-hand side of the ark on the front of these three boxes. Draw the shape on first and then paint it.

To assemble the ark, line the boxes up as shown below. Leave an opening between the two halves of the ark, so that the animals can process in, in a stately fashion, two by two.

During rehearsals, the actors should assemble the ark, by placing the boxes in the correct order. Attach loops of double-sided sticky tape to the sides of the boxes before the actual performance. This will ensure that when the actors assemble the ark on the night, it doesn't break up into separate boxes!

The Rainbow

The rainbow appears in the sky to Noah, during Act 2, scene 4. The simplest way to make the rainbow is to paint it on to a square piece of sheet (100cm by 100cm). Roll it up and suspend it from the flies. Unroll it when the rainbow appears.

The Waves

The dancers need several long pieces of thin material or crepe paper in blue and green to ripple up and down as the waves.

Small Props

A few small props are required. These should be placed on a props table off stage, ready for the actors to collect.

> Potatoes, and a peeler for Mrs Noah (Prologue/Act 1, scene 1)
> A pad, pencil and staff for Noah (Prologue/Act 1, scene 1)
> Spoons & forks for Rachel (Act 1, sc. 1)
> A scrubbing brush and a bucket for Rebecca (Act 1, sc. 1)
> A salt cellar, a jug and three cups for Ruth (Act 1, sc. 1)
> Rolled up plans for Noah (Act 1, sc. 2)
> Buckets of feed (Act 1, sc 2. and sc. 3 and also in Act 2, scene 2)
> An umbrella for Mrs Noah (Act 2, sc. 3)
> An olive twig for the Dove (Act 2, sc. 3)

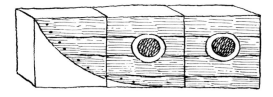

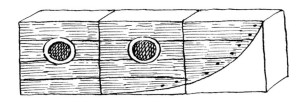

Lighting

Your school may own, or be able to hire, theatrical lighting. If so you will be able to follow the lighting instructions which are included in the text. But if not, it isn't vital to have special lights: many performances will take place in the daytime, in which case there is no need to use additional lighting.

However, if you are not planning to use theatrical lighting, you can always use the ceiling lights to good effect. Turn them off during scene changes and on and off again quickly during Act 2, scene 1 - the storm scene.

Casting and Auditions

Casting the Roles

First of all, I suggest you hold a meeting with all those interested in active participation (which may mean an awful lot of children). If you have decided to have a choir or dancers in the storm scene, as well as the cast, you can involve a very large number. But you may find there are too many children who are really keen to have major roles, and know that you can't accommodate everyone! If you find yourself in this situation, one way of dealing with it might be this.

Quieten the children down initially by telling them about the story of *Noah's Ark*. Then you could go on to talk about the characters in the play. You could show them the illustrations on pages 42-43 (The Main Characters). After that, you could explain to the children that anyone involved in the play will have to show a serious commitment.

They will have to take directions from the producer. Everyone will have to attend rehearsals regularly, and learn lines and songs. The children who opt for the main roles will have to do quite a lot of work to memorise their parts. At this stage, a number will privately decide that they'd rather be in the chorus after all! The beauty of *Noah's Ark* is that you can create as many small parts as you need.

Now you could mention the other enjoyable alternatives - being one of the dancers, or part of the choir, or orchestra. Announce forthcoming auditions for these as well as the speaking roles. Explain the important function of the stage management team (see page 44). It should be possible to include everyone in some way - and to let them know that they are *all* vital to the success of the performance.

Casting and Auditions

The Auditions

You may be an experienced producer, and have a clear idea of how to organise the auditions. If, on the other hand, you are new to this, the following suggestions for drama exercises might be useful. They should show you which children enjoy acting in this way, and can concentrate.

You will need to find a child with both stamina and charisma to play the part of Noah. There are usually one or two natural actors in a class. Look for the children who seem most comfortable with this kind of activity.

• First of all, settle the children down. Ask them to listen with their eyes shut as you describe the scene when the Storm Dancers create a storm and drown the Jeerers (Act 2, scene 1). Then ask the children to be the Storm Dancers, and to show you how the storm builds up, then gradually dies away.

• Next, let them try acting as animals. Ask the children to decide whether they are reptiles, birds, or other mammals. They should show you how their animal moves, eats, makes noises and goes to sleep.

• Make them work in pairs. Ask them to improvise the part of the scene when God first speaks and then appears to Noah (the Prologue). Ask them to show you how God makes an entrance and Noah's shocked reaction. Then they swop roles. This should help you to identify Noah.

• Get the children to sit and concentrate with their eyes shut once more as you describe the ark building scene (Act 1, scene 2). Ask them to imagine how it would feel to be doing such heavy work in the heat of the midday sun. Can they tell you what sort of activities might be going on? (E.g. sawing, hammering, painting, etc.) Tell them about the characters in that scene.

• Finally, divide the children into groups of six. Each group should include two of Noah's sons, two of their wives and two Jeerers. Ask them to improvise that scene, with Noah's family hard at work, and the Jeerers standing scornfully by. At your given signal, the rain begins to fall. Ask the children to show your their reactions, while remaining in character.

At this point, you could hand out scripts for a 'read-through' the next day. At the read-though, divide the children into groups. Give the children the chance to try reading in two or three scenes before making your decision about the main speaking parts.

The Main Characters

Mrs Noah
A sharp-tongued, practical woman. Houseproud. Kind-hearted. Very loyal to Noah.

Noah
An old man with great sense of purpose. Has undying faith in God.

Ham
The second son.
The joker of the family.

Shem
The oldest son.
A bit hot-headed.

Japheth
The youngest son. Practical.
Has a good head for figures.

God
All-knowing. All-seeing.
Omnipotent.

Ruth
Shem's wife. A calm, sensible girl.
A feminist before her time.

Rachel
Ham's wife. A lively girl,
with a sense of humour.

Rebecca
Married to Japheth. Slightly put upon.
She has a tendency to moan.

The Jeerers
A nasty bunch. Unpleasant hecklers who
come to a watery end.

The Stage Management Team

The stage management team should consist of about seven children. Their contribution is very important and they will need to attend rehearsals as well.

Members of the team can be given as many of these jobs as you judge to be necessary.

Scene Shifters
At least two members of the team are responsible for putting up the backdrop and taking large props on and off stage during scene changes. They could also be responsible for displaying the rainbow from the flies.

Props Table
One person should organise the props table. The props should be laid out ready for the actors to collect prior to their entrance. The props should be assembled on the table before the start of each act.

Lighting
If theatrical lighting is being used, an adult will be in charge of this. If you are using ceiling lights, a member of the team could turn the lights on and off during scene changes and at other appropriate moments. He or she should have a playscript, with their cues marked on it.

Prompter
The prompter should be supplied with a copy of the playscript and positioned inconspicuously - close enough to the actors to be able to prompt them easily if it's necessary.

Front Of House
At least two people can be given the responsibility for organising the seating and ushering the audience to their seats. They might enjoy making and handing out programmes as well.

Sound Effects
Two members of the team could make the sound effects (see page 48). They will need a copy of the playscript each, with their cues highlighted.

Director's Assistant
A very important person indeed. He or she will be your gofer, acting as messenger, reminder-in-chief and maker of cups of tea for you.

Rehearsal Schedule

Once the play has been cast, you will need to draw up a schedule. When will you be able to rehearse? Within lesson time or after school? A plan is necessary - with dates for the final run through and dress rehearsal scheduled in.

One tip - try not to get bogged down in the early stages, making each scene perfect before tackling the next - you may run out of time to finish. Keep moving onward; you will find that the whole play comes together later on.

Costume

If you don't already have a wardrobe of costumes at your school, don't worry; the costumes for *Noah's Ark* are easy to find or make. Beg or borrow some nightshirts, leggings, T-shirts and leotards to form the basis of the actors' costumes. Alternatively, the actors can wear simple tunics which can be made from almost any thin material. Sandals or flip-flops would be suitable for all the human characters in the play, and gym shoes for the animal characters. You could encourage the actors to decorate their costumes or to make their own masks, headdresses or hats.

Male Roles

Noah

Noah would look authentic in an oversized striped nightshirt, leggings, and leather sandals. Or he could wear a tunic in a natural colour worn over a T-shirt, belted at the waist with cord. Give him a beard with face paints (and add one or two wrinkles at the corners of his eyes). He needs a long knotted stick to use as his staff.

Shem, Ham and Japheth

All three boys could wear large, striped, shirts over leggings. Or, if they are available, oversized tracksuit trousers with elasticated ankles make excellent harem trousers. Team these up with brightly coloured T-shirts and short waistcoats. Make sashes to tie around their waists from plain scarves.

Shem, as the oldest son, would look very fine in a turban. Place a scarf at the back of the actor's head, cross over the ends at the front, and tuck them in. Pin on a brooch for further effect.

Female Roles

Mrs Noah

Mrs Noah is, and needs to look like, the boss. You could make her a tunic to wear over a T-shirt and tights, or she could wear a long dress in a bright colour. She should wear an apron.

Ruth, Rebecca and Rachel

You could give Mrs Noah's daughters-in-law a layered look. Two three-quarter length skirts worn on top of each other will create a nice fullness. Combine the two skirts with a leotard top, or T-shirt, and tie a patterned scarf around the waist for another layer. They could also wear plain scarves around their heads.

Costume

Unisex Roles

God

The actor playing God can wear a white tunic, or nightshirt. To make a splendid mask, cut out a circle from card, 70cm in diameter. Then cut it into a sunburst shape. Paint it yellow. Remove a circle for the actor's face. Attach the mask to a stick, so that the actor can hold the mask up to his/her face and look through.

The Jeerers

This lot are the biblical equivalent of lager louts! They should look distinctly disreputable. Give them an empty bottle to pass around and swig from.

The Storm Dancers

Blue, green or black leggings or tights and long-sleeved tops or leotards will form the basis of the Storm Dancers' costumes. Decorate these with circles and ribbons of blue and green tissue paper.

The Animals

The bottom layer of the animals' costumes will be T-shirts and leggings or leotards and tights in appropriate colours. But there are lots of distinctive touches that can be added to their costumes to make them look individual.

The Raven and the Dove

The Raven should (of course) wear black, and the Dove white. You can make a simple headdress for each bird. Cut out a strip of black or white sugar paper, 65cm long, and 10cm wide. Hold the two ends of the strip as shown, and fasten them together with clear tape. Fold along the dotted line to make the bird's beak, and stick on adhesive circles for the eyes.

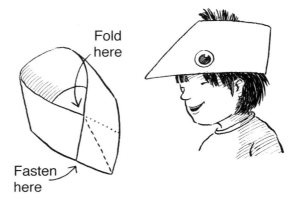

Fold here

Fasten here

The Tigers

The actors could make half masks (these leave the nose and mouth uncovered) using the template shown below. Adapt the shape to fit the individual child's face and mark where the eyeholes should be. Cut out the shape from thin card. Cut out the eyeholes and paint on markings. Attach elastic to the mask to fasten it.

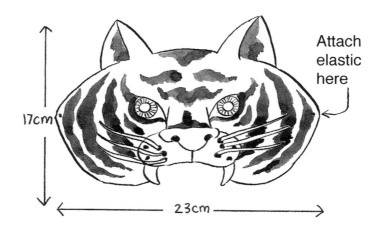

Attach elastic here

17cm

23cm

Costume

The Lions

Use the tiger mask template on page 46. Adapt and cut out the mask shape from light brown card. Place it on a sheet of yellow crepe paper, and cut out a shaggy mane to stick around the top of the mask. Attach elastic to the mask to fasten it.

The Crocodiles

Cut out the mask shape shown below. Fold back all the long strips and staple them together to fit at the back of the actor's head. This mask sits on top of the head. Fix elastic to go under the actor's chin to keep the mask in place. Fold along the dotted lines so that the crocodile's teeth can be seen.

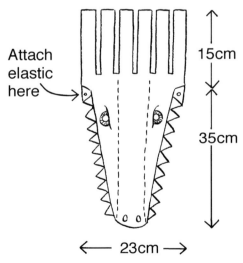

Attach elastic here

15cm

35cm

←— 23cm —→

The Snakes

The actors playing snakes could cut out green and red diamond-shaped scales from adhesive-backed plastic, and stick them on to dark leggings and leotards.

The Giraffes

Similarly, the actors playing giraffes could stick nicely-shaped brown spots on to light-coloured leggings and tops.

The Elephants

The elephants are easily identifiable by their ears. Make a headband to attach them to, by cutting a strip of thin card, 4cm wide by 60cm long. Fit it to the actor's head, and staple the ends together. Staple large floppy elephant ears made from crepe paper to it.

The Rabbits

Make a headband as described above. Cut another strip of thin card, and attach it to the headband, to fit across the top of the actor's head, from ear to ear. Stick two card rabbits' ears to the crossband.

The Frogs

You can make eye masks for the frogs using children's plastic spectacles.

To make the mask shape, first draw round the lenses of the sunglasses, so the the eventual eye holes on the mask will line up with the lenses. Draw the frog eyes on the paper mask. Remove circles from the middle of the eyes, so the actor can see through the mask. Attach the paper mask to the spectacles with little pieces of Blu-Tack.

Music

There are various ways that you can tackle the songs in the play. You may be an experienced music teacher and wish to write your own songs. You might like to use the songs that are included in the playscript (which are written to fit well-known traditional tunes). The songs can be accompanied on the piano or guitar.

You may prefer to incorporate songs that the children already know. If you have enough children, it is a good idea to have a choir. Some of the actors will be required to sing (while remaining in character) and will be aided by the choir's support.

There are three points in the play when taped classical music could be played: when the audience sees the completed ark, when the animals arrive and come aboard, and during the storm scene. The opening bars of Richard Strauss's 'Thus Spake Zarathustra' would be appropriate to show off the completed ark. Almost any march could accompany the animals' parade. 'Night on a Bare Mountain' by Mussorgsky might be suitable music for the storm scene. But of course, you might prefer to choose your own music.

Sound Effects

There are only a few sound effects in this play. Here are some suggestions as to how you could make them.

Thunder rumbling = a drum roll
A thunderclap = a clash of cymbals
Rain falling = shake rainmakers
A fanfare = two or three kazoos

Dances

There is only one dance called for during the play, and it takes place at the end of Act 2, scene 1. The Storm Dancers represent the waves of the sea and 'drown' the Jeerers. You might like to give the dancers lengths of material to ripple up and down as waves. Whether this is a simple piece of movement, or a more elaborately choreographed dance, it would be worthwhile to devote some time to a movement rehearsal - to polish the dance, and the animals' entrance into the ark during the previous scene.

If you wish to include more dances in the play, you can invent a simple dance to accompany the song, 'We've Reached the Shore' (Act 2, scene 3). The actors could link their arms, and step out and kick in time to the rhythm in a simplified can-can. If you have some talented dancers in your school, you could create short solos for the Raven and the Dove (Act 2, scene 2 - just before each bird flies away from the ark in search of land.)

Last of All...

Before the big night, keep as calm as possible, smile, and tell the children how great they're going to be. Try to remember that it's supposed to be enjoyable! When the children take their bows at the end and you see their glowing faces before you collapse with exhaustion and relief - that's when you'll realise that - actually - it was!

Break a leg!